Usborne

Fairytale Sticker Stories

Illustrated by Stephen Cartwright

Retold by Heather Amery

Edited by Laura Howell
and Sarah Khan

How to use this book

This book tells five fairytales. Some words in the stories have
been replaced by pictures. Find the stickers that match these
pictures and stick them over the top. Each sticker has
the word with it to help you read the story.

Some of the big pictures have pieces missing. Find the stickers with
the missing pieces and stick them down to finish the pictures.

A yellow duck is hidden in every picture. When you have found
the duck you can put a ⬤ sticker on the page.

Cover design by Michael Hill   Digital manipulation by Keith Furnival

This edition first published in 2007 by Usborne Publishing Ltd, Usborne House, 83-85 Saffron Hill, London EC1N 8RT, England.
www.usborne.com Copyright © 2007 Usborne Publishing Ltd. The name Usborne and the devices ♔ 🎈 are Trade Marks of Usborne
Publishing Ltd. All rights reserved. No part of this publication may be reproduced, stored in a retrieval system, or transmitted in any
form or by any means, electronic, mechanical, photocopying, recording or otherwise without the prior permission of the publisher.
First published in America 2007. U.E. Printed in Malaysia.

Contents

Sleeping Beauty

Once there was a good King and Queen.

After many years, the  had a baby

girl. The  and Queen were delighted,

and loved the little Princess very much.

6

The baby Princess was christened.

Six good  came to a feast at the royal palace. But the  forgot to ask the seventh fairy, who was cruel and wicked.

fairies

King

I found the duck!

Five of the fairies made good wishes.

The sixth  fairy was about to make

her wish for the little  baby . Suddenly

the wicked fairy appeared, looking very angry.

8

"The Princess will die," she said.

"She'll prick her  on a spinning wheel."

finger

"No," said the good . "I wish that

fairy

she won't die, but will sleep for a hundred years."

9

The Queen cried and the King shouted.

"All spinning wheels in my kingdom must

be burned," said the

King

. "Then the

Princess will never prick her on one."

finger

10

The Princess grew up in the palace.

When she was seventeen, she had a Grand

Birthday Ball. The good  came to

fairies

the Ball. They had all forgotten the  .

wicked fairy

11

Next day, the Princess found a staircase.

It led to a little room she had never seen before.

Inside was an old woman with a .

spinning wheel

It was the  in disguise.

wicked fairy

I found the duck!

"What are you doing?" said the Princess.

"I'm spinning, my dear. Come closer, and I'll

show you," said the old woman. The

Princess

put out her  and pricked her finger.

hand

13

At once, she fell fast asleep.

Everyone else in the  went to sleep

palace

too. The six good fairies carried the Princess to

her  . The wicked fairy vanished.

14

bed

Nothing moved in the palace.

I found the duck!

Everything was still and silent for a hundred

years. A thick  grew around the

forest

palace. The good  watched over it.

fairies

15

One day, a young Prince came by.

He saw the roof of the palace and asked an old

man about it. "A  sleeps in there,"

Princess

said the  , "but there's no way in."

old man

The Prince walked to the palace.

The trees moved apart and let him through. He

ran past the sleeping
guards
, up the steps

and through the
doors
. It was very quiet.

17

He found the Princess fast asleep.

She was so beautiful, he kissed her gently. The

Princess

opened her eyes and smiled. "At last,

a handsome  to save me," she said.

Prince

18

Everyone in the palace woke up.

"I'm hungry," said the . "Tonight

Queen

we'll have a great feast," and she thanked the

 for saving everyone.

Prince

19

The Prince wanted to marry the Princess.

"Of course," said the . The Prince and

King

Princess

got married, and the good fairies

were invited. They all lived happily ever after.

20

Little Red Riding Hood

Everyone liked Little Red Riding Hood.

I found the duck!

She lived with her mother near a forest. Her

name came from the bright red

cloak

with a that her Granny made for her.

hood

"Your Granny isn't feeling well."

"Please take her this basket of   .

food

Go through the forest, but don't talk to

strangers," said Red Riding Hood's

mother   .

23

Red Riding Hood set off.

She skipped along with her  .

basket

Red Riding Hood didn't see a big, bad

 watching her from behind a tree.

Wolf

24

Out jumped the Wolf.

"Where are you going,  ?" asked

Red Riding Hood

the Wolf. "I'm taking this basket of food to my

Granny's  in the forest," she said.

cottage

25

"How kind you are!" said the Wolf.

I found the duck!

He smiled a horrible smile. "Why not pick

some flowers for her too?"  was

Red Riding Hood

a little scared. "Yes, Mr. Wolf," she said.

26

Red Riding Hood put down her basket.

I found the duck!

She picked a big bunch of flowers . The

Wolf ran down the path to Granny's

cottage. He was very, very hungry.

The Wolf found Granny's cottage.

He knocked on the 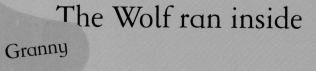. "Come in, my

door

dear!" called Granny The Wolf ran inside

and gobbled her up in one big gulp.

28

He climbed into Granny's bed.

The Wolf put on Granny's nightcap and

glasses. He pulled the covers up to his

chin, and waited for  to come.

Red Riding Hood

29

Soon, the Wolf heard Red Riding Hood.

I found the duck!

She knocked on the  . "Come in,

door

my dear!" said the Wolf, in a squeaky voice.

"I'm here in my  ."

30

bed

"Hello, Granny," said Red Riding Hood.

Then she stared. "Why, Granny, what big

eyes

you have!" she said. "All the better

to see you with," squeaked the

Wolf

Red Riding Hood felt very scared.

I found the duck!

"But, Granny, what big [ears] you have!" said Red Riding Hood. "All the better to

hear you with," squeaked the Wolf.

32

"And, Granny, what big teeth you have!"

"All the better to EAT you with!" said the

 and jumped out of  . Red

Riding Hood screamed, but the Wolf ate her up.

33

A woodsman heard the scream.

"I'd better see if the old lady needs help," said the

woodsman

. He ran to Granny's

cottage

as fast as he could. The Wolf was asleep.

34

The woodsman killed the Wolf.

 and Red Riding Hood were inside the

Granny

Wolf. The woodsman used his knife to let

them out. They were very happy to be rescued.

"Thank you for saving us!" said Granny.

I found the duck!

"The 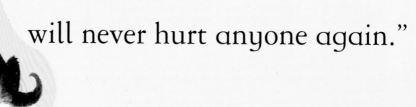 will never hurt anyone again."

Wolf

The woodsman dragged the Wolf away

and they all sat down to tea and cake

36

Three Little Pigs

A Mother pig had three baby pigs.

They all lived in a little . One

house

day,  said, "You're too big for my

Mother Pig

house. It's time you had houses of your own."

38

I found the duck!

"Goodbye," called . "Build

Mother Pig

good houses, but never open the

door

to the Big Bad Wolf. He'll gobble you up."

39

The first little Pig met a man.

The  man had a bundle of straw. "May I

please have some straw to build a house?" said

the  little Pig . "Yes, you can," said the man.

The little Pig worked hard.

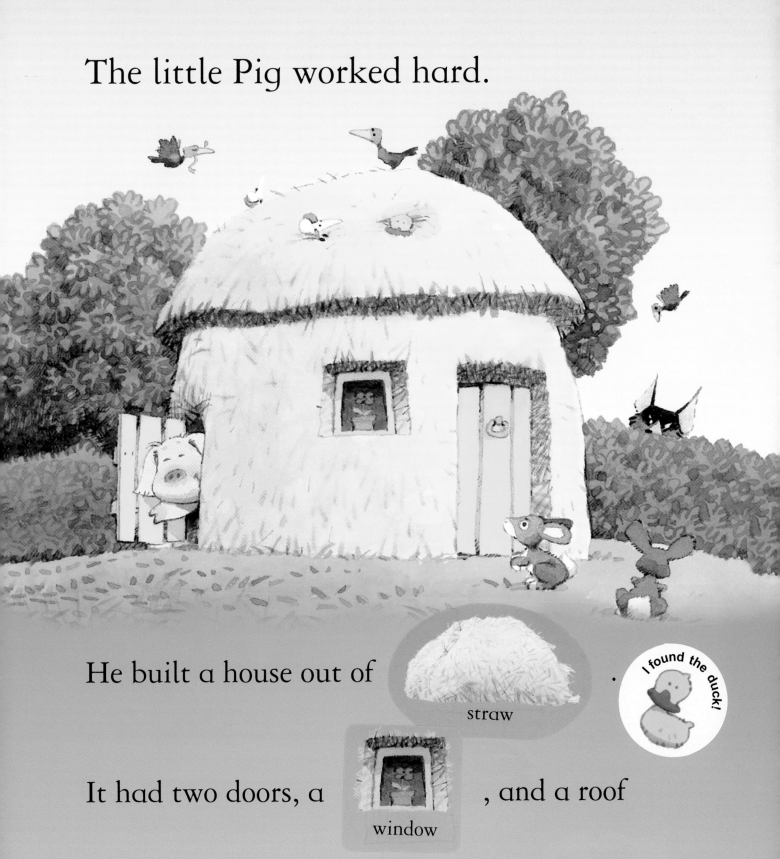

He built a house out of straw.

It had two doors, a window, and a roof

on top. "I'll be safe in here," said the little Pig.

I found the duck!

The second little Pig also met a man.

This man had a bundle of sticks. "May I please

have some  to build a house?" said

sticks

the  "Yes, you can," said the man.

little
Pig

42

The little Pig worked all day.

He made his house from sticks. It had two doors,

strong walls and a  around it. "This

fence

will keep the  out!" said the little Pig.

Big Bad Wolf

43

The third little Pig met another man.

This man had a pile of bricks. "May I please

have some  to build a house?" said

bricks

the  . "Yes, you can," said the man.

little Pig

The little Pig worked for many days.

He built a **brick house** with thick walls,

two windows and a tall **chimney** "I'm not

afraid of the Big Bad Wolf!" said the little Pig.

45

The Wolf came to the straw house.

"Let me in," he said to the , "or

little
Pig

I'll huff and puff and blow your house down."

And he blew the  down.

straw house

46

The little Pig ran to the stick house.

The two  hid behind the curtains.

little
Pigs

"Let me in," said the  . "No, no,

Big Bad Wolf

we won't let you in," said the two little Pigs.

I found the duck!

47

The Wolf huffed and puffed.

The
stick house
fell down. The two little Pigs

ran to the brick house. "Let me in," said the

Big Bad Wolf
, "or I'll blow your house down."

48

"We won't let you in," said the little Pigs.

The Big Bad Wolf huffed and puffed, but the

brick house

stayed up. He looked for a way in.

The Pigs watched through the  .

window

49

The Wolf jumped onto the roof.

He looked down the . The three

little Pigs put a big  of water on

chimney

pot

the stove. "Now we're ready," said the Pigs.

The Wolf slid down the chimney.

He fell into the  with a splash.

pot

The little Pigs put on the 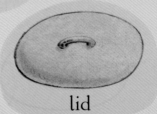 . "That's

lid

the end of the Big Bad Wolf!" they cheered.

51

All three Pigs stayed in the brick house.

"Time for supper," said the third little pig.

They drank of coffee, happy that the

 would never frighten them again.

Goldilocks
and the
Three Bears

I found the duck!

Once there were Three Bears.

I found the duck!

They lived in a cottage in the middle of the woods. Father Bear was big, Mother Bear was middle-sized, and Baby Bear was tiny.

54

One day, Mother Bear made porridge.

But the  was too hot to eat.

porridge

"Let's go for a walk while it cools," said Father

Bear. And they went out of the  .

cottage

I found the duck!

A naughty girl named Goldilocks came.

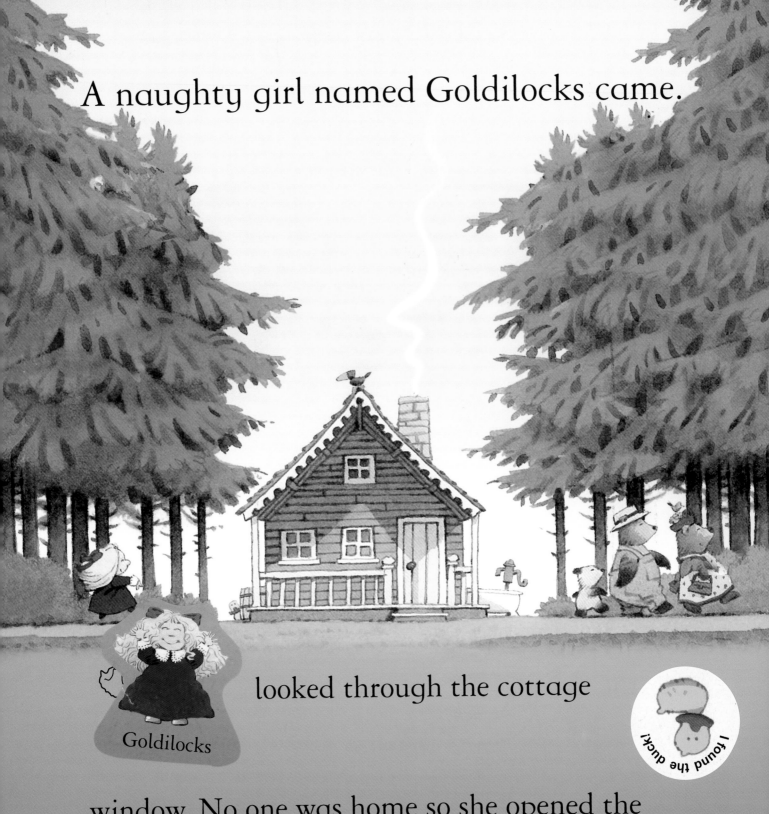

Goldilocks

looked through the cottage

window. No one was home so she opened the

and stepped inside.

door

I found the duck!

She saw the three bowls of porridge

She tried them all. "That porridge is too hot," said  Goldilocks, "That one is too cold. This  porridge is just right." And she ate it all up.

Goldilocks felt sleepy.

She sat on a chair. It belonged to  Father Bear .

"It's too hard," she said. She tried another. It

belonged to  Mother Bear . "It's too soft," she said.

Goldilocks sat on the smallest chair.

I found the duck!

It belonged to  Baby Bear . "This is just right,"

she said. Then there was a loud crack. The chair

broke into pieces and  Goldilocks fell.

59

Goldilocks went into the bedroom.

She lay on a  bed. It belonged to Father

Bear. "It's too high," she said. She tried one that

belonged to  Mother Bear. "It's too low," she said.

60

Goldilocks lay on the smallest bed.

It belonged to  Baby Bear . "This is just right,"

she said. Soon she was fast asleep. She didn't hear

the Three Bears come into the  cottage .

61

The Three Bears wanted their porridge.

Father Bear said, "Who's been eating my

porridge

?" "And who's been eating my

porridge?" said

Mother Bear

.

62

Baby Bear looked at his bowl.

"Who's been eating my  porridge ? And

they've eaten it all up," he said. He put down

his spoon and started to cry.

63

Father Bear looked around the room.

"Someone's been in here," he said.

looked at the crumpled 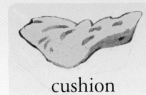 on his chair.

cushion

Father Bear

"Who's been sitting in my chair?" he said.

Mother Bear looked at her chair.

"And who's been sitting in my chair ?"

said Mother Bear. "Who's been sitting in my chair,

and broken it all up?" said Baby Bear .

The Three Bears went into the bedroom.

"Who's been sleeping in my  ?"

bed

said  "And who's been sleeping

Father
Bear

in my bed?" said Mother Bear.

66

Baby Bear looked at his bed.

"Who's been sleeping in my bed? And, look,

she's still in it," said  . Just then,

Baby
Bear

 woke up. She was very scared.

Goldilocks

67

Goldilocks jumped out of bed.

She rushed out of the  and ran home

cottage

to her mother as fast as her legs would carry her.

The  never saw Goldilocks again.

Cinderella

Cinderella was very sad.

She watched her wicked Stepmother and ugly

Stepsisters through the  . They always

window

left  behind when they went out.

70

Cinderella

They made Cinderella work all day.

She scrubbed the floor with a  and

cooked the meals. She slept in a cold, creepy room

with bare floors and an old wooden  .

71

They all had invitations to a Royal Ball.

The two ugly  ripped open their

Stepsisters

invitations

. They were very excited. "We must buy

new dresses, and look our best!" they squealed.

It was the day of the Ball.

The Stepsisters put on their ,

dresses

ready for the Ball. "May I come too?" asked

Cinderella . "NO, NO, NO!" they shouted.

Cinderella sat down and cried.

Suddenly, her Fairy Godmother appeared. She

had wings, and a magic wand. "Do as I say, and

you shall go to the Ball," said the

Fairy Godmother

74

"Bring me these things."

Cinderella brought the Fairy Godmother a

pumpkin, six white  , a brown

mice

rat, and six green lizards in a  .

basket

75

The Fairy Godmother waved her wand.

In a flash, the pumpkin became a coach,

the mice were horses, the rat was

a coachman, and the lizards were footmen.

Cinderella had a pretty dress and shoes.

"Cinderella, you must leave the Ball before the

clock

strikes midnight or the magic

will fade away," warned the .

77

Fairy Godmother

Cinderella went to the palace.

The Prince met her at the door. Everyone

thought that  was a princess. She

Cinderella

had a lovely time dancing with the  .

Prince

Suddenly, the clock struck twelve.

"It's midnight. I must go!" cried Cinderella.

She ran down the palace 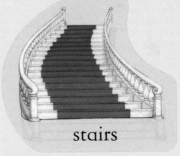 so fast

stairs

that one of her  fell off.

shoes

Cinderella ran all the way home.

She sat on a  stool in the kitchen in her

old rags. When the  Stepsisters came home,

they told Cinderella all about the Princess.

80

Next day, the Prince was very unhappy.

He wanted to find the Princess. A footman

brought him her  shoe . "I'll marry the girl

who can wear this shoe," said the  Prince

The Stepsisters tried on the shoe.

They pushed and pulled. They screamed and

cried. But the  had big, ugly feet.

Stepsisters

The  was much too small for them.

shoe

82

"May I try the shoe?" asked Cinderella.

Of course, the shoe was a perfect fit. As if by

magic, the  appeared. She changed

Fairy Godmother

Cinderella's rags into the pretty  .

dress

83

"I have found you at last!"

"Will you marry me?" asked the Prince

"Yes!" said Cinderella. They were married the

very next day, and lived happily ever after.